For all people who call
Louis Armstrong
"Brother"
OH YEAH!

# WHAT A WONDERFUL WORLD

## illustrated by ASHLEY BRYAN

PUPPET SHOW TODAY

SATCHMO

by George David Weiss and Bob Thiele

A Jean Karl Book

ATHENEUM BOOKS FOR YOUNG READERS

I see trees of green,

red roses too,

I see them bloom

for me and you,

and I think to myself,

"What a wonderful world!"

I see skies of blue

and clouds of white,

the bright, blessed day,

the dark, sacred night,

and I think to myself,

"What a wonderful world!"

The colors of the rainbow,
so pretty in the sky

are also on the faces
of people going by.

I see friends shaking hands,
saying, "How do you do?"

They're really saying,
"I love you."

I hear babies cry,

I watch them grow.

They'll learn much more

than I'll ever know,

and I think to myself,

"What a wonderful world!"

Yes, I think to myself,
"What a wonderful world!"

Atheneum Books for Young Readers
An imprint of Simon & Schuster Children's Publishing Division
1230 Avenue of the Americas
New York, NY  10020

The illustrations are tempera and gouache paintings.

First edition

Printed in the United States of America

10  9  8  7  6  5  4  3  2  1

ISBN 0-689-80087-8
Library of Congress Catalog Card Number: 94-78123